If You're Happy and You Know It

Illustrated by Melanie Mitchell

Published by Sequoia Children's Publishing,
a division of Phoenix International Publications, Inc.

8501 West Higgins Road
Chicago, Illinois 60631

59 Gloucester Place
London W1U 8JJ

www.sequoiakidsbooks.com

10 9 8 7 6 5 4 3 2

ISBN 978-1-64269-039-2

If you're happy and you know it, clap your hands.
If you're happy and you know it, clap your hands.
If you're happy and you know it, then your face will surely show it,
If you're happy and you know it, clap your hands!

If you're happy and you know it, wag your tail.
If you're happy and you know it, wag your tail.
If you're happy and you know it, then your tail will surely show it,
If you're happy and you know it, wag your tail!

If you're happy and you know it, stamp your hooves.
If you're happy and you know it, stamp your hooves.
If you're happy and you know it, then your hooves will surely show it,
If you're happy and you know it, stamp your hooves!

If you're happy and you know it, give a roar.

If you're happy and you know it, give a roar.

If you're happy and you know it, then your roar will surely show it,

If you're happy and you know it, give a roar!

If you're happy and you know it, hop around.

If you're happy and you know it, hop around.

If you're happy and you know it, then your hop will surely show it,

If you're happy and you know it, hop around!

If you're happy and you know it, wave your trunk.
If you're happy and you know it, wave your trunk.
If you're happy and you know it, then your trunk will surely show it,
If you're happy and you know it, wave your trunk!

If you're happy and you know it, roll around.

If you're happy and you know it, roll around.

If you're happy and you know it, then your roll will surely show it,

If you're happy and you know it, roll around!

If you're happy and you know it, shout hooray!
If you're happy and you know it, shout hooray!
If you're happy and you know it, then your shout will surely show it,
If you're happy and you know it, shout hooray!